Zac Strikes Out
published in 2014 by
Hardie Grant Egmont
Ground Floor, Building 1, 658 Church Street
Richmond, Victoria 3121, Australia
www.hardiegrantegmont.com.au

A CiP record for this title is available from the National Library of Australia.

Illustrations by Tomomi Sarafov
Design by Stephanie Spartels

Printed in Australia by Griffin Press, an Accredited ISO AS/NZS
14001:2004 Environmental Management System printer.

3 5 7 9 10 8 6 4 2

The paper this book is printed on is certified against the
Forest Stewardship Council® Standards. Griffin Press holds
FSC chain of custody certification SGS-COC-005088. FSC
promotes environmentally responsible, socially beneficial
and economically viable management of the world's forests.

ZAC STRIKES OUT

BY H.I. LARRY

ILLUSTRATIONS BY **TOMOMI SARAFOV**

hardie grant EGMONT

CHAPTER

Zac Power was walking down the street. It was really hot. He was going to get an ice-cream.

Zac was 12 years old. He was a spy. It was top-secret work.

Zac worked for a spy group called GIB. His code name was Agent Rock Star.

GIB sent Zac on missions against enemy spies. They also sent him to Spy Camp.
He learnt cool things there, like sky-diving.

Zac stopped at a crossing.
He looked at the traffic lights.

The red man turned into a green man. But this green man was different. He looked like Zac!

That's weird, thought Zac. The traffic lights flashed.

Suddenly a rope dropped at Zac's feet. He looked up.

The rope was coming from a GIB chopper. Its propeller looked like a giant ninja star.

Zac climbed up the rope to

the chopper. There was

no-one at the controls. *It must*

be on auto-pilot, thought Zac.

The chopper's screen flashed.

Flying to Spy Camp.

Zac took out his SpyPad.

Every GIB spy had a SpyPad.
It was a phone and a computer
in one. It had heaps of
apps and cool games.

Zac played a game on his
SpyPad.

Suddenly the chopper's screen flashed.

You are at Spy Camp.

The chopper landed with a bump.

CHAPTER 2

Spy Camp was a silver
dome. There was a canteen
in the middle.

A big TV screen was
hanging from the roof.

The TV screen showed the GIB Spy Ladder. When GIB spies finished missions, they got points. They also got points for doing Spy Camp tests.

Zac had been at the top of the Spy Ladder lots of times.

GIB SPY LADDER

1. *Agent Rock Star*
2. *Agent Wave*
3. *Agent Pizza Breath*
4. *Agent Speedway*

Zac collected his Info-Disk from the front desk. It had all his Spy Camp information on it. Zac put the Info-Disk into his SpyPad.

Spy Camp Skill:
Karate

Training Buddy:
Agent Small Fry

Training Place:
Black Mountain

Black Mountain? thought Zac.

That's where Agent Ice Storm

lives! He had read about

Agent Ice Storm. She was

the world champion in karate.

People said she was super scary.

'Excuse me,' said someone,

tapping Zac on the shoulder.

Zac turned around. A small boy

looked up at him.

'Wow, it's really you!' said
the boy. 'I'm Lucas...I mean,
Agent Small Fry.'

'Hi, I'm Zac,' said Zac.

'I know,' said Lucas. 'You're,
like, the coolest spy ever!'

'Well, I don't know about that,' smiled Zac. 'But thanks. Let's get ready!'

Zac and Lucas found the Karate room. This was where their karate gear was stored. They scanned the lock with their SpyPads.

The door opened. There were two white karate suits inside. Zac and Lucas put the suits on.

Zac picked up a gadget box from a shelf. There was a round keyring inside. It had a spider painted on it.

Zac read the label on the box.

Magnetic Web

Traps anything.
Press the button and a
spider web comes out.

Zac put the Magnetic Web onto his karate belt. There was one for Lucas too.

'Let's go,' said Zac. 'We can take the chopper that flew me to Spy Camp.'

They ran outside and got into the chopper.

'Can I fly?' Zac asked Lucas. 'I know the way to Black Mountain.'

Lucas nodded. Zac turned off the auto-pilot and took off.

'I've heard Agent Ice Storm
can karate chop through
metal,' said Lucas.

'I've heard she does karate in
her sleep!' said Zac.

Lucas looked scared.

'Maybe she's not as scary as people say,' said Zac.

'I hope not!' said Lucas.

CHAPTER 3

Zac flew above the clouds.

Lucas is a bit shy, he thought.
I wonder if he'll be good at karate.

Soon Zac could see the top of

Black Mountain.

It was covered with snow.

As they got closer, Zac saw a building. It had a big staircase and the roof was made of gold. There was a place for the chopper to land.

They landed and Zac and Lucas got out. It was freezing! There was snow everywhere.

Agent Ice Storm walked towards them.

She had long black hair and was very tall. Her white karate suit looked just like Zac's. 'Follow me!' she yelled.

They ran up the stairs to a big hall.

The floor was covered in mats. There were swords hanging on the walls.

'Get ready for karate training,' said Agent Ice Storm. 'You'll practise hard and then be tested. The test results will give you points for the Spy Ladder.'

Agent Ice Storm walked over to a block of wood.

'HEE-YAH!' yelled Agent Ice Storm. She chopped the wood in half with her hand.

'Strength is important for karate,' said Agent Ice Storm. 'Zac, you start on the Muscle-Tron.'

Agent Ice Storm pointed to a machine. It had arms coming out of it. Zac pressed the start button.

The machine's arms pushed against Zac's body. He had to push them away. He felt all his muscles getting stronger.

Lucas used the Muscle-Tron too.

Then they practised karate chops. Zac broke through foam and a big block of soap. So did Lucas.

'You're good, Lucas,' said Zac.

'Thanks,' said Lucas. His face went red.

'Time for self-defence,' said Agent Ice Storm. 'GIB spies don't start fights. But we must know how to defend ourselves.'

Zac put on a helmet and chest pads. They had sensors on them.

Zac and Lucas had to protect their head and chest from being hit by Agent Ice Storm.

Lucas went first. He was really fast.

Then Zac had his turn. He dodged and blocked nearly all of Agent Ice Storm's kicks and punches.

'Good job, agents,' said Agent Ice Storm.

She wasn't as scary as Zac
thought she would be.

'It's time for the test,' said
Agent Ice Storm.

Zac and Lucas followed her
outside into the snow.

CHAPTER

Zac saw two robots in the

snow. They were tall and

white. Agent Ice Storm

turned the robots on.

Their eyes lit up.

'These are Snowbots,' said Agent Ice Storm. 'Most robots freeze in cold places. But Snowbots work, even in the snow. They will run two tests for you.'

'One test will be on self-defence and one will be on strength,' Agent Ice Storm added. 'Good luck!'

Agent Ice Storm went inside.

'Start self-defence test,' said Zac's Snowbot in a robot voice.

The Snowbot swung its leg at Zac's head. Zac ducked out of the way.

The Snowbot punched at Zac's chest. Zac blocked it with his arm.

SMACK!

Then the Snowbot tried to karate chop Zac's head. Zac ducked again. He was awesome!

After a while, Zac's Snowbot stopped.

'Self-defence test over,' said the Snowbot. 'Start strength test.' The Snowbot picked up a block of ice.

'Destroy the ice,' said Zac's Snowbot.

Zac took a deep breath.

'HEE-YAH!' he yelled.

He slammed his hand onto the ice-block. The ice-block broke into pieces!

Zac's Snowbot picked up a piece of wood. It looked very strong.

'Destroy the wood,' said the Snowbot.

Zac lifted his hand up and hit the wood.

THUNK!

The wood didn't break.

'OUCH!' yelled Zac.

He looked at Lucas.

Lucas was about to hit his own block of wood.

SMASH!

It broke in half!

'That was awesome!' said Zac.

Suddenly, Lucas's Snowbot
pushed Lucas into the snow.

'Destroy Agent Small Fry,'
said the Snowbot.

CHAPTER 5

'Watch out!' yelled Zac.

Lucas rolled out of the way.
Zac ran over and helped
Lucas up. The Snowbot
attacked Lucas again.

Lucas blocked the Snowbot's kicks and punches.

POW! SMACK!

'I'm getting tired, Zac,' said Lucas. 'I can't fight much longer!'

Zac jumped in front of the Snowbot. It threw two quick punches at Zac. He ducked and the Snowbot missed.

Suddenly Zac remembered
the Magnetic Web.
He unclipped it from his belt
and pressed the button.

A metal net sprang out and
covered the Snowbot.

It was trapped!

Zac stopped to catch his breath. 'That was crazy!' he said.

'I know,' said Lucas. 'Thanks for your help.'

Zac ran back to his Snowbot. It was still holding the wood for Zac to chop.

Zac yelled louder than ever and hit the wood.

SMASH!

The wood broke in half and fell onto the snow.

Agent Ice Storm came out of the building.

'The Snowbot attacked Agent Small Fry!' said Zac.

Agent Ice Storm looked shocked. 'It's lucky you're a black belt in karate, Agent Small Fry,' she said.

'Really?' said Zac. 'You're a black belt?'

Lucas went red. 'You thought of using the Magnetic Web,' he said.

'Well done, agents,' said Agent Ice Storm. 'I'll fix the Snowbot while you head back to Spy Camp. Your test results will be sent there.'

CHAPTER

Zac and Lucas got into the
chopper. They flew back to
Spy Camp. Lucas wasn't as shy
this time. He chatted to Zac
the whole way.

'Lucas, why didn't you say you were awesome at karate?' asked Zac.

Lucas shrugged. 'I didn't want to show off,' he said.

When they got back to Spy Camp they went to the canteen. Zac got a Rocky Road ice-cream. Lucas got chocolate.

Zac's SpyPad beeped. It was his test results.

Great self-defence

and strength.

10 points.

Zac looked up at the Spy

Ladder. He was still on top.

He looked at Lucas's name.

'Look, Lucas,' said Zac. You're number four. That's awesome.' He gave Lucas a high five.

'Cool,' said Lucas. His cheeks turned red again. But this time he looked happy.

> **GIB SPY LADDER**
>
> **1. Agent Rock Star**
> **2. Agent Wave**
> **3. Agent Pizza Breath**
> **4. Agent Small Fry**

THE END